THE CULTURE OF CLOTHES

A TEMPLAR BOOK

This edition published in the UK in 2024 by Templar Books.
First published in the UK in 2021 by Templar Books,
an imprint of Bonnier Books UK
4th Floor, Victoria House
Bloomsbury Square, London WC1B 4DA
Owned by Bonnier Books
Sveavägen 56, Stockholm, Sweden
www.bonnierbooks.co.uk

Text copyright © 2021 by Giovanna Alessio
Illustration copyright © 2021 by Chaaya Prabhat
Design copyright © 2021 by Templar Books

1 3 5 7 9 10 8 6 4 2

All rights reserved

ISBN 978-1-80078-926-5

This book was typeset in Mostra Nuova and Beloved Sans
The illustrations were created digitally

Edited by Isobel Boston and Carly Blake
Designed by Adam Allori
Production by Emma Kidd and Giulia Caparrelli
Consultant: John Gillow

Printed in China

THE CULTURE OF CLOTHES

WRITTEN BY GIOVANNA ALESSIO
ILLUSTRATED BY CHAAYA PRABHAT

templar
books

A Journey Around the World's Clothes

Traditional clothing is worn by people all over the world as a celebration of their cultural identity. In some countries, traditional dress is still worn on a daily basis. In others, people only wear their traditional clothes for special occasions, such as festivals or birthdays. The style, material and colour of this clothing can speak volumes about the wearer and their culture – from where they live, to what their role in society is and what their beliefs are.

In this book, you'll travel across oceans and continents to take a closer look at some of the most fascinating examples of traditional dress. From the Quechua women in Peru who record the history of their culture by embroidering it on their clothing, to the Bamileke people in western Cameroon who wear beaded elephant masks to honour their ancestors, discover how people use clothing to celebrate their cultural identity.

As the world becomes ever more connected, styles of clothing change and develop, and the important visual language of traditional clothing is in danger of getting lost. This book has been created to showcase the rich variety of clothing around the world and to celebrate the cultures who wear them.

So what makes up traditional dress?

Colours

From glittering gold sashes to ruby red feathers, cultures use colours to represent everything from the wearer's social status to their religious beliefs.

Adornments

It's not just clothing such as shirts or trousers that make up traditional dress. Cultures add a multitude of adornments to their traditional clothing, from gold jewellery to carved pendants. These items have great significance to the wearer and can sometimes be many generations old.

Materials

In the past, cultures around the world used local materials to create clothing to suit their needs – whether to protect the wearer from freezing temperatures or simply to showcase the riches of their culture. Today many cultures still use these distinctive materials to create their traditional dress.

Inspiration

For thousands of years, cultures have taken inspiration from world around them to create their clothing. Traditional dress is often embroidered with floral designs and decorated with symbolic items, such as the feathers of prized birds. Local legends and history also play an important part in the development of clothing. In many parts of the world, traditional dress is worn by people at festivals and events to preserve and celebrate the history of their culture.

CONTENTS

ASIA · 8

- CHINA — LONGHORN MIAO — 10
- BALI — OLEG DANCER — 12
- PHILIPPINES — IFUGAO MAN — 14
- JAPAN — RYUSOU ACTOR — 16
- INDIA — BANJARA WOMAN — 18
- THAILAND — PAMEE AKHA — 20
- SIBERIA — TUVAN SHAMAN — 22
- SOUTH KOREA — TRADITIONAL HANBOK — 24

NORTH AMERICA · 26

- MEXICO — TEHUANA WOMAN — 28
- GREENLAND — WEST GREENLAND TRADITIONAL DRESS — 30
- USA — SIOUX GRASS DANCER — 32

SOUTH AMERICA · 34

- BRAZIL — BAIANA DE ACARAJÉ — 36
- PERU — QUECHUA WOMAN — 38
- ARGENTINA — GAUCHO COWBOY — 40
- PANAMA — POLLERA DRESS — 42

EUROPE · 44

SPAIN — FLAMENCO DANCER — 46
CZECH REPUBLIC — KROJ FOLK COSTUME — 48
NORWAY — HARDANGER BUNAD — 50
PORTUGAL — LAVRADEIRA DRESS — 52
GERMANY — BAVARIAN LEDERHOSEN — 54
FRANCE — ALSATIAN DRESS — 56
SCOTLAND — HIGHLAND KILT — 58

AFRICA · 60

NIGERIA — YORUBA DANCER — 62
MALI — FULANI WOMAN — 64
KENYA — MAASAI WARRIOR — 66
NAMIBIA — HERERO WOMAN — 68
CAMEROON — BAMILEKE MASQUERADE DANCER — 70

OCEANIA · 72

NEW ZEALAND — MĀORI WARRIOR — 74
PAPUA NEW GUINEA — HULI WIGMAN — 76
SAMOA — TAUPOU DANCER — 78

ASIA

As the world's largest continent, Asia stretches over a staggering 45 million square kilometres. It is here that Mount Everest, Earth's highest peak, towers 8,850 metres over the valleys of Tibet and the Dead Sea. It is also here where Earth's lowest point can be found, dipping more than 400 metres below sea level near the dry hills of Jerusalem.

Due to its wide reach, encompassing every conceivable kind of landscape, the people of Asia have found an astounding array of ways to clothe themselves. From the yak-wool cloaks of the Siberian Tuvan to the cooling wide-sleeves of the Japanese kimono, this vast continent offers a rich variety of traditional dress.

CHINA

Longhorn Miao

In southwest China's Guizhou province live millions of people known as the Miao. One small Miao community that numbers just 5,000 people lives in a sprinkling of villages on the sides of the mountains around a town called Longga. They are called Longhorn Miao and are known for celebrating the annual flower festival of the Lunar New Year in spectacular style.

During the festival, the Longhorn Miao women wear a special costume made up of a vibrantly decorated shirt embroidered with white flowers and a pleated skirt patterned with pink and orange stripes. As the Miao didn't traditionally have a written language, these designs have been used to record their people's history, including tales of war.

Yet it is what the Miao women wear on their heads that makes this traditional dress particularly notable: a gigantic headdress made mostly of human hair. The Longhorn Miao's ancestors believed that wearing the headdress would frighten off any wild beasts they might encounter in their remote mountain villages. Putting the headdress on is a complex task. First, a horn-shaped frame is attached to the wearer's head, then a collection of yarn, wool and human hair is wrapped around the frame and held in place with a white ribbon. The headdresses are never taken apart – instead, they are passed down from generation to generation. Some of the hair can be hundreds of years old, representing a lasting link between the Miao and their ancestors.

Women collect their hair from hairbrushes and add it to their headdresses. Some can weigh as much as 4kg.

The patterns on the Miao women's shirts and skirts are created using a knife dipped in hot wax.

Girls learn to embroider at age 6 or 7. Being able to create special patterns is considered a sign of intelligence within the community.

BALI

Oleg Dancer

From volcanic mountains shooting skyward to waters that shimmer shades of aquamarine blue, Bali packs so much natural beauty into an island just 150 kilometres wide. The vibrant culture of the Balinese people is just as rich, with an ancient tradition of dance forming an important part of it. Balinese dancers wear clothing to depict themselves as queens, gods, animals and supernatural creatures, and apply makeup to their faces to exaggerate their transformations. Once reserved for religious rituals on this ancient island, today these dances are performed mostly to entertain.

Some of the most elaborate costumes in Bali are worn by female Oleg dancers, whose performance is also known as 'the dance of the bumblebees'. From head to toe, the dancers are adorned with gold. Dressing begins by wrapping a long sash, called a *sabuk*, around the dancer's torso. A cloth covers the bottom half of the dancer's body, covered in gold patterns and edged with pompoms and adornments. Large gold bracelets decorate their wrists and arms.

On the Oleg dancers' heads sparkle exquisite golden crowns. These crowns, called *gelungan*, are decorated with tiny golden sandat flowers, which sway gently as the dancer's arms shiver in tiny, trembling movements that represent bees collecting nectar.

The sash is wrapped tightly around the dancer and is believed to represent the one the dancer loves, wrapping their arms around her in an embrace.

Heavy gold bracelets represent the fact that the dancer never loses control of their hands, for example to steal things.

As running is considered to look ridiculous in Balinese culture, the dancer's skirt is pulled tight to her body to encourage her to take smaller steps.

PHILIPPINES

Ifugao Man

For the last 2,000 years, the Ifugao people have harvested rice on lush green terraces that inch up the mountains of Luzon, the largest island of the Philippines. It makes sense that the Ifugao are farmers, since their name translates to 'people of the earth'. During ancient ceremonies and rituals, though, it is the skies, not the land, they look towards.

During these ceremonies, male spiritual leaders called shamans wear elaborate headdresses. These impressive pieces are decorated with feathers, wild pig tusks or the beaks of hornbill birds, which the Ifugao believe are able to carry messages to the gods. Traditionally, the top half of the body is either bare or wrapped loosely in a blanket, but the rectangular piece of coloured cloth that covers their lower body is full of symbolism.

Diamond patterns on the lower cloth are said to represent ferns, one of the planet's oldest plants, to commemorate the Ifugao's ancestors. Stars represent a god who is the child of the Sun and the Moon, and helixes (double spirals) represent the lightning god, who also carries messages to other divinities. Yet it is a lizard that is one of the most distinctive symbols on the traditional dress. This design is thought to bring wealth and good fortune, because it is believed that a monitor lizard was sent by the gods to teach the Ifugao how to grow rice high in the mountains.

The strings that dangle from a bag called a moma are used to count the number of days an Ifugao man has worked. A knot is tied for each day of labour.

The cloth, called an uloh, has several uses. At night it's used as a blanket and by day it's wrapped around the shoulders for protection, or used to carry things.

The Ifugao use their long spear for a variety of purposes. On some occasions it is used as walking stick, on others it is used for hunting or as a defensive weapon.

JAPAN

Ryusou Actor

In the humid temperatures of Okinawa, a Japanese island located between the East China and Philippine seas, it's important to have lightweight clothing to keep the wearer cool. With its thin, billowing cloth and wide sleeves, the traditional Ryusou kimono has been prized by the inhabitants of Okinawa for hundreds of years.

The Ryusou kimono is painted in brilliant hues of golden yellow and bright red, colours that symbolise the island. By wearing this kimono, today's Okinawans continue a tradition dating back hundreds of years, to when the island was an independent nation known as the Kingdom of Ryukyu. During this time, the Ryusou kimono was worn by members of the royal family and other nobility. The most common designs from the Ryukyu era, known as *bingata*, featured natural world elements, such as animals, flowers and trees.

Today, the kimono is usually worn for special occasions, such as graduation ceremonies or weddings. But Okinawans performing classical Ryusou plays wear the traditional dress as well. These actors complete their outfit with exaggerated, oversized hats called *hanagasa*. Seemingly made of gigantic red petals, the hats are designed to resemble the hibiscus flower, a symbol of the island.

In the Ryukyu era, bingata designs were so labour-intensive to make that only the wealthiest families could afford them. Designs were kept under strict control, with some reserved for royalty.

The Ryusou kimono is tied at the waist with a belt called a minsaa.

Since both men and women used to dress alike in Japan, women adorned their hair with pins and silk flowers to look different.

INDIA

Banjara Woman

The Banjara, a group of semi-nomadic people found scattered across India, are renowned for their highly colourful textiles. Originally salt and grain merchants, the Banjara were constantly on the move and so adorned their clothing with embroideries and ornaments to act as talismans against bad fortune. Today, Banjara women still wear their traditional clothing on a daily basis as a symbol of their cultural identity.

Made from a patchwork of colourful fabric, the Banjara dress is as unique as it is beautiful. The clothing is heavily embroidered and comprises of three main elements: a *cholis* (a backless blouse), a *ghaghras* (a voluminous skirt) and an *odhani* (a long headscarf). It is further embellished with an abundance of coins, beads and mirrors. The use of mirrors is particularly distinctive for the Banjara and is believed to be a symbol of good fortune.

Banjara women are also known to add a multitude of symbolic ornaments to their bodies, from rings and chains, to heavy bangles that cover their arms. The quality and quantity of the jewellery reflects the wearer's position within the community. Textiles form a significant part of the Banjara's identity as a culture and their colourful traditional dress is designed to reflect their vibrant lifestyle. To this day, embroidered Banjara material can be found in bazaars across India and is sold throughout the world.

Banjara material is used for many different products – from bags and purses to clothing and cushion covers.

The odhani is made to be long enough to cover the Banjara women's backs. It is covered in shells, beads and mirrors.

A Banjara woman often wears up to 5kg worth of jewellery on a daily basis.

THAILAND

Pamee Akha

On the stretch of high jutting land that snakes across Thailand, as well as nearby parts of Burma, Laos, Vietnam and China, the groups of farming hill tribes known as the Akha live in stilted bamboo villages that cling to the low mountainsides.

The women who live in these distinctive villages wear their traditional dress on a daily basis and are recognised for their towering trapezoidal headdresses, called *u-coes*. Akha women decorate these caps with a multitude of silver ornaments, coins and buttons, which signify wealth within their community. The Akha are so proud of their headdresses that they even sleep wearing them.

Making clothing is considered a work of art in the Akha culture and is a great source of pride among the women in the community. Their traditional dress comprises of a short jacket, skirt and leggings – and each item is covered with embroidery, silver medallions, buttons and coins. One Akha tribe, known as the Pamee, painstakingly cross-stitch strips of brightly-coloured cloth and attach them in rows to their jackets. Although the Akha wear their traditional dress all year round, they reserve their best clothing for the annual Swing Festival in August. During this event, the villagers celebrate the end of the harvest and make pleas for a good crop next year. The women use this festival to showcase the clothing they have spent the year making – and the event is sometimes referred to as 'Women's New Year'.

Girls receive their first headdresses when they are 6 years old and ornaments to decorate them are given as birthday gifts each year.

Pamee embroidery and needlework is made up of geometric patterns, which are traditional in their culture.

When the headdress starts to droop from all the decorations, a bamboo frame can be added to help hold it up. Some headdresses can weigh over 5kg.

SIBERIA

Tuvan Shaman

Vast and often bitterly cold, Siberia stretches from the towering Ural Mountains to the point where the Pacific and Arctic Oceans meet. Though Siberia is nearly twice as big as Australia, just 33 million people live there, making it one of the most sparsely populated places on the planet. Among these hardy inhabitants are the tribe of herders and horsemen known as Tuvans.

The Tuvan people have lived nomadic lives for over a thousand years and today they can still be found across many different parts of Asia – from Xinjiang (China), to Outer Mongolia and Russia. Today, Tuvans still wear their traditional clothing on a daily basis. Silken robes with long sleeves are designed to protect their hands from the cold while they work and belts made of strips of silk are wrapped around the waist several times, to support their back during long days on horseback.

The most sacred Tuvan clothing is reserved for their religious leaders, called shamans. Shamans are regarded as mediums between the natural world and the spirit world and they are the most respected members of the Tuvan community. Every part of the shaman's clothing is symbolic – from their coats that are adorned with objects to ward off evil spirits, to the towering headdresses that teeter on the tops of their heads. Shamans prize birds they consider magical, such as the crow and the cuckoo. By topping their headdresses with the feathers of these birds, shamans believe they can channel the powers of these creatures.

To Tuvans, red is the colour of life. Felt socks usually have a rim of red at the top which peek above their boots.

Ancient Tuvan textiles includes needlework using golden thread. One of the designs is the olchei, or the eternity knot, which symbolises everlasting happiness.

Buttons usually don't fasten anything on Tuvan clothing and serve only as a decoration.

SOUTH KOREA

Traditional Hanbok

With a landscape of lush green hills dotted with ancient Buddhist temples, Korea was populated by nomads more than a thousand years ago. The loose silhouette of the Korean traditional costume, the hanbok, has changed very little over the past 2,000 years.

This traditional dress dates back to the Goguryeo Dynasty (37 BC – AD 668), which was one of the ancient Three Kingdoms of Korea. Historically, the colour and fabric a hanbok was made from reflected the wearer's social rank. Lower members of society could only wear cotton hanboks of white, a colour Koreans associated with purity, modesty, peace and patriotism. Members of the nobility wore luxurious, colourful hanboks made of silk. Royalty were the only people who could wear yellow, and gold was reserved strictly for emperors, as the Koreans believed the colour represented the centre of the universe. Today, hanboks of all colours and materials can be worn by every member of society.

The traditional hanbok consists of two main pieces: a short jacket called a *jeogori* and a long, billowing skirt called a *chima*. When the Mongol Empire ruled Korea in the 13th century, the *jeogori* was cut to above the waist and was tied with a long ribbon. However, by the late 19th century, the design was adjusted slightly. It was shortened up to the chest and was worn with a sash, following modern Chinese fashion.

The hanbok was worn every day until about 100 years ago, but today it is reserved for special occasions, weddings and New Year's Day.

The patterns embroidered on a hanbok trepresent the wishes and hopes of the wearer. For instance, pomegranates represent children.

A small purse is tucked into the waistband. It is made by gathering five folds of fabric and is often embroidered with natural elements, such as plums and lotus flowers.

North America

Positioned between the Atlantic and Pacific oceans, the sweeping continent of North America contains a wide variety of landscapes. Windswept plains meet rugged mountains in the far west, and in the south, bustling towns and cities bask in the blazing sunshine.

Indigenous cultures, such as that of the Maya people, and Native American tribes thrived on this continent. All of these cultures were inspired by natural wonders to create clothing that was both part of and a celebration of the land in which they lived. At least 5,000 years ago, the ancestors of Inuits carved out their home in the frozen north of this continent. Here, they used to furs and skins of Arctic animals to protect themselves against the freezing temperatures.

MEXICO

Tehuana Woman

The sun-warmed piece of land called Tehuantepec curls like a beckoning finger, connecting North and South America. In Tehuantepec, the culture is matriarchal, which means that the women are in charge of the town's finances and the markets. The region is famous for its *velas* – traditional festivals where women of all ages parade through the streets in their most flamboyant costume, the *tehuana*.

For hundreds of years, the *tehuana* has been a celebration of the social status, religious beliefs and wealth of the wearer. Made of two or three different layers, this vibrantly embroidered dress consists of a *huipil* (a straight rectangular top) and a huge A-line skirt that is gathered at the waist. The whole look is crowned with a headpiece of pleated fabrics, flowers and ribbons, known as the *Huipil Grande*.

Although *tehuana* costumes made from cotton and silk are worn every day, on festival days the women of this region don *tehuana* made of velvet. For these special occasions, flowers fashioned from silk thread are adorned with gold jewellery that have been passed down from generation to generation. This show of gold is not designed to demonstrate status or power, but rather to celebrate the importance of tradition and the strength of the women who live in this region.

The famous artist Frida Kahlo (1907–1954) wore the tehuana as a symbol of female empowerment.

The blouses are decorated first, then folded and sewn together with an opening left in the middle for the head.

A well-made huipil can be worn for 20 to 30 years. When it becomes too old to wear, it is cut into small pieces of cloth and sewn into a blanket.

Greenland

West Greenland Traditional Dress

Ice covers 85 per cent of the gargantuan island of Greenland, creating a vast, mostly frozen world. Yet in spite of the challenges of living in an ice-covered land, a group of nomadic hunters migrated to Greenland nearly 5,000 years ago and have thrived there ever since. Known as the Inuit, they protected their bodies from the extreme cold by wearing traditional clothing made from the skins of Arctic animals adapted to survive in this icy place.

The traditional Greenland dress is no longer used by Inuits on a daily basis, but it is worn with pride on special occasions – such as the first day of school and birthdays. The modern version of the dress is a riot of colour. The hoodless anorak, called a *timmiaq*, was traditionally made from animal skin, but today is made from cotton or silk and dyed a bright red. An elaborate collar is worn on top of the anorak and is adorned with glass beads in a variety of shapes, sizes and bright colours.

Embroidered trousers are cut short and reach the tops of tall, thick boots, called *kamikis*. These sealskin boots were originally designed to allow the wearer to easily travel through Greenland's ice-covered landscape on foot or dogsled. They are decorated with lace and a border of floral patterns. These intricate designs are often created using a traditional technique called *avittat* – where the pattern is made from pieces of dyed sealskin leather, cut into small strips and sewn together into beautiful designs.

Colourful glass beads were first brought to Greenland by the Dutch crews of whaling boats in the 17th century. They exchanged beads for help with hunting.

Though Inuits across the Arctic wear kamiks, only in Greenland are they decorated with silk threads and local floral patterns.

Traditionally, older women wear dark blue or yellow kamiks, and younger women wear red kamiks.

USA

Sioux Grass Dancer

With a mighty shaking of the Sioux grass dancer's body, the thick fringe on his costume swishes and sways, mimicking tall grass waving in the wind on the vast northern plains that spread across northwestern USA and into Canada. This is the home of the Sioux, one of the many Native American tribes.

Some believe the idea of the grass dance originated when young Sioux boys tied the grass to their clothing after stomping prairie ground to clear an area for a new camp. Others say the ancient Sioux wore rows of grass to camouflage themselves on the open prairie as they hunted buffalo or fought other tribes.

Today on the flat, grassy plains, many different groups of Native Americans gather at traditional powwow festivals to feast together and share dances that tell the stories of their tribes. Though many tribes are renowned for their intricate beadwork, none are more so than the Sioux. The grass dancer costume is made up of many different elements: armbands, a headband, breech cloth, a breastplate, fringed fabrics and tassels, and two strips of cloth called holsters that hang down each side of the belt. Each element of the outfit is designed to exaggerate the movements of the dance and all are intricately decorated in traditional Sioux style with floral or geometric beaded patterns.

To make jingling sounds as the dancers move, bells are attached to both ankles with leather straps.

Instead of attaching each bead separately, the Sioux often use a 'lazy stitch', stringing eight beads together before sewing them down.

Though some traditional Native American groups are known for their elaborate traditional headdresses, for the grass dancer there are just two eagle feathers that sway on top of a thick brush of porcupine quills on the dancer's head.

SOUTH AMERICA

South America is made up of towering mountains and kilometres of flat, pristine beaches. While today the continent is filled with modern cities that never seem to sleep, ancient civilisations such as the Inca Empire once thrived here, and remnants of their temples and cities remain.

In the chilly Andes Mountains, some cultures use embroidery and traditional dress to record the ancient stories of their people – each item of clothing filled with personal significance and meaning. On South America's sun-soaked shores, dancers twirl in costumes that display the histories and stories of their people for all to admire.

BRAZIL

Baiana De Acarajé

In the northeast of Brazil lies the state of Bahia, and on a small peninsula on its sun-kissed coast sits the town of Salvador. This town is famous for its vibrant celebrations and for the dazzling *Baiana de Acarajé* women, who can be spotted around the town dressed in their swirling white skirts and selling traditional Afro-Brazilian delicacies. Salvador is known for its vibrant carnival parties and when a day's selling ends, dancing in the streets begins.

Only the *Baianas* sell the tasty fried *acarajé* – a black-eyed-pea-and-shrimp fritter dish believed to have been created as an offering to Iansã, an African god of winds and storms. The *Baiana* women and their striking dress have become synonymous with the town's signature dish. The outfit itself is a blend of the *Baianas'* rich cultural heritage, with an abundance of colourful jewellery to reflect their African roots, and lace details which represent the influence of Portuguese colonial rule on the town.

Floor-length and voluminous, the *Baianas'* dress is made up of several layers of skirts, topped by a bodice that dips below the waist. Both items are white, in honour of the white-robed Oxalá, one of the deities of the Afro-Brazilian religion, Candomblé. On the *Baianas'* head is a long piece of muslin cloth, wrapped around several times to form a headscarf. Their arms, ears and neck are bursting with stacks of bangles, beaded necklaces and earrings, all in hues so bright they seem to rival the Brazilian sun.

Even though summer temperatures can exceed 40°C, Baianas sometimes cover their dress with a white shawl called a singue.

The lace on the bodice of the dress is lovingly embroidered by hand.

White cotton pantaloons, called calçolão, *are worn underneath the full skirts.*

PERU

Quechua Woman

The Quechua people live in villages that cling to the cool, high-up slopes of the Andes Mountains in Peru. They are known for their exceptional fabric-making skills, but weaving is more than just their livelihood – the fabrics they make act as a record of the Quechua's cultural history. They weave the stories of their people into the cloth, which they then cut and shape into clothing. The Quechua don't traditionally have a written language and this practice began thousands of years ago as a record of everything from local traditions to personal experiences.

The clothing that the Quechua women weave is passed on from one generation to the next. Creating textiles is such an integral part of their culture that children learn to weave by three or four years old. There is symbolism in every pattern on their clothing, from stories of folk heroes to depictions of the natural world. For women's clothing in particular, every inch of the bright fabric is covered in a kaleidoscope of stories – each painstakingly embroidered by hand.

The Quechua's clothing has practical uses, too. A large decorative piece of cloth, called an *lliclla*, is worn as a shawl to keep their shoulders covered and warm, or it can be used to carry heavy loads. It is common for a Quechua woman to wear layer upon layer of embroidered skirts to protect herself from the elements. But it is the hat, called a *monteras*, which is the most unique part of their traditional dress. Held in place by delicate woven straps, this distinctive headwear is brightly coloured and is adorned with an exquisite array of white beads, sequins and floral patterns.

Yarn to make the fabrics is made from sheep, alpaca or llama wool, and is dyed using local plants, minerals and insects.

The elaborately decorated jackets worn by Quechua women are turned inside out for everyday use to protect the designs from damage as they go about their work.

Quechua women usually wear several skirts at once, and on special occasions may wear up to 10 or 15 at a time.

ARGENTINA

Gaucho Cowboy

Across the Pampas, the rolling plains that sweep more than 750,000 square kilometres from the Atlantic coast west to the Andes Mountains, cowboys called gauchos can be found going about their business of herding cattle. Gauchos have become a symbol of national pride in Argentina, inspiring songs and epic poems about their nomadic lifestyle.

The name gaucho comes from the South American Indian word for 'outcast', but these skilled horsemen have chosen to live solitary lives on the plains for hundreds of years. Gauchos live and work on vast ranches, tending to their horses and looking after herds of cattle. Their uniform has been the same for at least 300 years – a white shirt with a short, open jacket, a wide-brimmed hat, and a handkerchief tied in a knot at their neck. Their loose-fitting cotton trousers, called *bombachas*, and high leather boots are designed to be comfortable and durable to withstand long rides across the Argentinian grasslands.

When the temperature in the shadow of the Andes Mountains drops, gauchos wear thick woollen ponchos around their shoulders to keep the cold weather at bay. In the past, the poncho also served as a saddle bag and a blanket for protection during winter nights. Today, Argentina is home to more than 150,000 gauchos, who still live and work on the vast plains.

A useful gaucho tool is a boleadora, a mass of stones bound with leather strips, that the gaucho throws at the legs of runaway cattle.

Spurs made of iron are worn on the heel of each leather boot to help direct their horses.

The national flower of Argentina, a ceibo, is sometimes used to decorate clothing and other gaucho items.

PANAMA

Pollera Dress

Over the past 400 years, Panamanian women have transformed the pollera costume into an art form that represents their nation. Each year during carnival season, the streets of Panama are filled with women swirling and dancing in the sunshine – all dressed in the traditional pollera costume.

At first glance, the pollera appears to be made up of millions of tiny pleats. As the wearer twirls, the pleats unfold, creating a seemingly endless swathe of fabric. Though it appears to be a dress, the pollera can be broken down into two parts. It consists of a ruffled blouse and an enormous gathered skirt, called a *pollerón*, from which the costume gets its name. Some skirts are all white, while others are more colourful, decorated with lace, crochet and embroidery. An abundance of gold jewellery, most often including gold rosary beads, is worn around the neck.

Gold combs and intricate beaded hairpins are worn on the dancer's head in some regions of Panama. In other regions, the pins are replaced by a delicate crown of wire flowers called a *tembleque*. These headpieces are expertly decorated with golden or silver filigree (intricately crafted wire). True to their name, the crowns are designed to tremble with even the slightest movement, and quake when the festival dancing begins.

Tembleques, gold necklaces, pearls and other accessories are passed down from generation to generation.

Women usually only have two pollera skirts during their lifetime: one before the age of 16 and the other for adulthood.

The colourful wool pompoms on the back of the pollera are called motas *or* bellotas.

Europe

From the icy fjords of Scandinavia at its northern fringe, to the shimmering seas at its southern shores and the lofty Alpine peaks in between, Europe is packed with natural wonders of every kind. Yet it is not just astounding geographical variety that makes this region so exciting to explore.

Europe might be the second-smallest continent in the world, but it is a rich patchwork of different languages and cultures. Although this continent has a history of kings and queens, the design of its traditional clothing often celebrates the importance of ordinary people.

SPAIN

Flamenco Dancer

Dotted with palm trees and bathed in Mediterranean sunshine, Seville sits in a region of southern Spain known as Andalusia. It is here on the lush banks of the Guadalquivir River that the passionate dance known as the flamenco came into existence.

A flamenco dancer, standing tall and proud in her traditional dress, curls her arms above her head, preparing to dance. Accompanied by the gentle music of a guitar, she slowly swoops her arms up and down, snapping her fingers in time to the beat. She raises each leg in turn, billowing the ruffles below her knees. When her feet flick down again, her shoes crash against the floor, creating a rhythmic set of sharp taps.

For this display, the flamenco dancer wears a dress that mirrors the shape of a guitar, slender at the top and falling in rows of ruffles to floor. The flamenco dress originated as a robe worn by the local Roma people, known as *gitanos*, as they went about their daily chores. The Roma began wearing these robes to special events in 1929, embellished with ruffles and fashioned in bright colours. Soon after, the flamenco was established as the official dress of Andalusia. Today, the flamenco dress is worn by women in this region at traditional festivals and events as a show of Andalusian pride.

The typical fabric for the dress is polka dotted, although it can also be floral printed or a plain colour.

Other accessories can include earrings, necklaces, castanets and a fan made of cloth or wood.

Flamenco shoes are made of leather with rubber soles. They have a nail at the toe and another at the heel to create sharp tapping sounds during the dance.

CZECH REPUBLIC

Kroj Folk Costume

Hidden among the green hills of the Czech Republic in Central Europe sits the farming town of Vlčnov. Although it is small, Vlčnoc is renowned for its elaborate female folk costume, known as *kroj*. Although this costume is also worn as a symbol of local pride, it is the outfit's significance at Vlčnov's annual Ride of Kings festival that makes it so unique.

Swaddled in ribbons and ruffles, women in their *kroj* outfits are elaborately dressed from their head to their toes. Billowing pleated sleeves envelop their upper arms and vibrant embroidery, tassels and lace cover their dresses. On their heads they wear an extravagant headdress, decorated with flowers and ribbons.

Local legends claim that in 1469 in the Kingdom of Bohemia (now part of the modern-day Czech Republic), the King's son-in-law tried to usurp the throne. When he failed to overthrow the King, the son-in-law escaped, disguised in the female *kroj* costume so he wouldn't be recognised and captured. Each year at the Ride of Kings festival, a young man is chosen to represent the son-in-law and parades through the town on horseback, wearing the *kroj*. He is surrounded by a procession of page boys who are also dressed in the folk costume. Even their horses are dressed for the occasion – decorated with ribbons and colourful paper flowers. Each year, crowds of spectators gather together to celebrate the legend of this small town.

It is common to wear three or more petticoats under the kroj *to get the required 'bell shape' of the skirt.*

The boys in the the parade tuck flags into their boots to celebrate their town.

The woollen material is embroidered with local floral designs and sequins.

Norway

Hardanger Bunad

The country of Norway sits at the very tip of mainland Europe, its edges jagged from deep fjords and towering cliffs. When summer breaks on these often ice-covered lands, and when 17 May arrives (Norway's National Day), Norwegians celebrate their culture by dressing in an embroidered *bunad*, the traditional folk dress of their country.

Since a bunad's colour and decoration is specific to each town and village, there are a few hundred local varieties, perhaps as many as 400. Arguably the most famous is the *bunad* from the Hardanger region, known for its bold coloured skirt and sparkling white apron, topped by a red wool vest and an embroidered breastplate. Either a cap or headscarf is worn on the head. Traditionally, caps are worn by young women, with headscarves reserved for married women. The headscarf on the *Hardanger Bunad* must have exactly 250 pleats.

A multitude of silver accessories decorate this signature outfit, including a neckpin and brooch, to hold the shirt together, cufflinks, shoe buckles and belts. Norwegian folklore tells of the mines deep beneath Norway that belonged to mythical creatures called trolls, who were master silversmiths. In the past, silver accessories were worn as talismans against bad weather and to heal illnesses, and were passed down from one generation to the next.

Jewellrey is usually stamped, cast or cut from silver sheets and embellished with engravings.

Historically, the colours of the embroidery revealed the marital status of the wearer. White embroidery meant the wearer was single and multicolored meant the wearer was married.

Black shoes and stockings are worn to complete the outfit.

PORTUGAL

Lavradeira Dress

Snaking down Europe's westernmost edge, Portugal sits alongside the Atlantic Ocean. Each year, hundreds of Portuguese men, women and children gather at a religious festival called the Feast of Our Lady of Agony. Held in the small coastal town of Viana do Castelo, this week-long event is the largest traditional festival in Portugal and celebrates the enduring connection between the Portuguese and the sea.

One of the most iconic outfits that can be seen at the festival is the lavradeira folk costume. Though the costume originated from traditional farming dress, the lavradeira has become one of the most celebrated folk costumes in Portugal. On the wearer's head is a fringed piece of fabric called a kerchief, pulled back to provide a colourful backdrop for large gold earrings. During festivals, it is traditional for women to show their wealth and adorn themselves with gold jewellery, often many generations old. A multitude of medallions, heart-shaped charms and heavy chains are pinned to their shoulders.

The bodice is worn over a white shirt, intricately embroidered with blue floral designs. The voluminous skirt below usually sweeps the floor, but some women shorten it during the festival for dancing. The apron on top is hand-woven from thick wool and is liberally decorated with local designs and embroideries. On their feet, the dancers wear low-heeled backless slippers, called *chinelas*.

A separate ornamental pocket called an algibeira, usually in the shape of a heart, is tucked into the bodice.

There are two different colour designs for this costume. The red dress is worn by young women or on happy occasions, such as weddings. Blue or green costumes are worn by older women, or on sad occasions.

When the outfit first originated in the 17th century the designs were simple and geometric, but in 1918 a local painter started a trend of using more elaborate floral motifs.

GERMANY

Bavarian Lederhosen

From the snow-capped Alps to the vast lakes and forests, Bavaria is as rugged a landscape as they come. The region's traditional dress, the lederhosen, was originally based on the working clothes of 16th century farmers, but this practical costume has evolved dramatically over the last five hundred years.

Made of thick, durable leather, lederhosen shorts were first used in the 16th century to distinguish the peasant class from the higher ranks of society, such as merchants, knights and lords. Two and a half centuries later, a Bavarian prince called Luitpold upset this tradition by choosing to wear lederhosen himself. His gesture transformed the lederhosen into a symbol of pride in Bavaria and today the traditional costume is still worn at cultural events, such as Oktoberfest. At this festival, which lasts for several weeks, people of all ages gather together to celebrate Bavarian culture.

Lederhosen shorts are usually worn with knee-high socks and shirts with horn buttons. Leather braces, a traditional jacket known as a *lodenjacke* and a pointed felt hat topped with pheasant or rooster feathers completes the outfit. The lederhosen is generously embroidered and each element of the costume celebrates local nature, even down to the shape of the wearer's shoes, called *haferlschuhe*, which are said to have been inspired by a goat's hoof.

Literally translated to leather (leder) trousers (hosen), legends claim that they should never be washed to maintain their softness.

The colourful embroidery on the shorts and braces traditionally signifies the village where the wearer is from.

The lederhosen are sometimes adorned with a chain across the top of the flap, called a charivari, that can be decorated with charms thought to bring luck.

FRANCE

Alsatian Dress

The picturesque region of Alsace stretches from the Vosges Mountains in the west to the Rhine River in the east. Although Alsace is now part of France, its borders have not always been clear and the region has been passed between French and German control several times over the past three hundred years. The traditional Alsatian dress is an outfit that, like summer in Alsace, contains a riot of colour: white, green and brilliant red, considered by the Alsatians to be the colour of fire and life itself.

The traditional dress is usually worn at summer festivals and for religious pilgrimages called *Pardon*. It is made up of a white cotton shirt, with a lace-knitted collar and a long skirt. In the past, the colour of the Alsatian skirt varied depending on the religion of the wearer. Catholic women wore a long red skirt called a *kutt*, while Protestant women wore the *rock*, a shorter skirt of green, blue, red or purple. A bodice and apron is usually worn over the skirt, covered with ribbons and local floral designs.

The most distinctive part of the Alsatian traditional dress is the extravagant headdress, known as the *coiffe*. These bonnets can reach over one metre in diameter and are decorated with silver and gold sequins, small pieces of glass, or even stones from the nearby Rhine River. *Coiffes* were originally modest caps, designed to protect the wearer from unpredictable weather along the rocky sea coasts of France. Over time, however, they evolved into elaborate designs – with their shapes representing everything from the wearer's home village to how they made living. Today the traditional *coiffe* is still worn with pride by young women at festivals all over France.

The long ties of the apron wrap around the back to be tied into an elaborate bow.

A square or rounded colarette, which is knitted or made of linen with a lace border, covers the open collar of the blouse.

Traditionally, the colour of the headdress a woman wore reflected her religious beliefs. Protestants wore black ribbons, while red and multicoloured ribbons were worn by Catholics.

SCOTLAND

Highland Kilt

Scotland may be part of the same landmass as England, but this small country has a very proud and distinctive culture. It also has one of the most instantly recognisable forms of national dress in the world: the kilt. Family ties are extremely important to the Scots and their surnames traditionally reflect their family's history. This sense of pride is reflected in their national clothing – and each family has their own unique tartan design (a colourful, criss-cross pattern), which is featured on their kilts.

In the 16th century, the kilt was used as a simple blanket or cloak, to protect the wearer during the cold Scottish winters. It was called the *féile-breacan*, or the 'great kilt' and was around six metres long. Wool was the material of choice for the kilt, not only because it was plentiful in Scotland, but because the heavy fabric retained heat and kept the wearer warm and dry in the unpredictable Scottish weather.

Over the centuries, the kilt has developed from a plain and practical garment into a decorated and celebrated piece of clothing. Today, modern Scots still wear their traditional kilts for special events and as a celebration of national pride. For these events, the kilt is accompanied with a white shirt, dark jacket and a square of tartan called a fly plaid, which is pinned to the wearer's left shoulder. Stockings, flat leather shoes and an abundance of silver accessories complete this traditional dress.

Though originally just folded and belted, today kilts have exactly 29 pleats and are made using 7m of fabric.

Kilts don't have pockets, so a small leather pouch called a sporran is attached to the belt.

A kilt knife, often with a decorative handle, is often kept tucked inside the top of the long stockings.

AFRICA

The world's very first humans evolved in Africa about seven million years ago and humans have been living there ever since. Since most parts of this continent are very hot and very dry, many of Africa's people were traditionally nomads, living their lives on the move and following the rains to find good soil and grazing.

The African people share this untameable place with some of Earth's most majestic creatures, including giraffes, lions and elephants. Taking inspiration from these animals' natural adornments, Africans have long found ingenious ways to clothe their bodies. Traditionally they dressed for ease of movement and to keep cool, but their clothing also has great significance to their many different cultures, from giving the wearer the ability to summon the spirits of their ancestors to the power to transform into an elephant.

NIGERIA

Yoruba Dancer

For more than 1,500 years, the Yoruba people have lived on the sun-baked plains of Nigeria in Western Africa. Many Yoruba are farmers, producing everything from grains to cacao seeds. Others are craftspeople, including leather workers, glass-blowers and wood carvers. Although today the Yoruba number nearly 20 million, one thread that connects them all is a deep respect for their ancestors.

Nigeria's *Egungun* masquerade festival is a centuries-old Yoruba tradition, and one of the most colourful cultural celebrations in Western and Central Africa. During this unique festival, *Egungun* dancers dress in elaborate and otherworldly clothing – and are believed to take on the physical form of the spirits of their ancestors. The celebrations can stretch over several weeks and the event is accompanied by drumming, dancing and singing.

Masked and cloaked to the very tips of their toes, performers in the *Egungun* festivals hide their entire bodies, so there is no sign of the human form underneath. As the dancer spins, stomps and swoops, the layers of fabric fan out, representing their ancestors returning to Earth to visit the living. The glass and beads scattered across the cloth are designed to reflect sunlight – making flashes of light to signal the spirit world. Each individual piece of decoration is believed to contain great power and is meaningful to the wearer.

Some outfits have screens of cowrie shells across the face. This allows the dancers to see out, but prevents the audience from seeing them. It is considered to be bad luck if you see the dancer's eyes.

Some designs feature animals such as rams, eagles, lions and elephants, which are all ancient Yoruba symbols of royal power.

Velvet, metal threads, sequins, beads and leather are items that the Yoruba find powerful and are signs of respect to their ancestors.

MALI

Fulani Woman

The Fulani people live spread across the sweltering expanse of West Africa, from Mali to Nigeria, Cameroon, Sudan and Guinea. They are traditionally nomadic, moving from one place to the next according to the needs of their community and the natural resources available to them. Though their clothing styles vary from region to region, it is a love of beauty and adornments that link this culture.

All Fulani share a love of things glittering and golden. Women decorate their bright clothing with precious beads, thick bracelets and anklets of gold. Heavy earrings called *dibi*, made of gold and hammered paper-thin, dangle from their ears and are a distinguishing feature of the Fulani traditional dress. Over time, more gold is added to a Fulani woman's earrings to indicate her wealth or status. The Fulani adorn themselves to the tops of their heads, braiding their hair with cloth, jewellery, amber beads, cowrie shells and even coins.

Marking their skin with tattoos is considered to be a form of lasting beauty for the Fulani and the tradition of tattooing lips, known as *Tchoodi*, is a common practice among women in the community. As young girls, the Fulani begin colouring their mouths with small lines using a hot needle, so by the time they reach adulthood their lips are completely black. This distinctive tattoo is designed to highlight the beauty of the Fulani's teeth and bright smile, and is a symbol of the courage and strength of the women in this culture.

Although they don't have a single design for their traditional dress, the Fulani wear bright clothing decorated with local geometric designs.

Fulani women do not tattoo their top lip until they get married. The tattoo is made using a hot, thin needle and a special natural ink.

Red rope is often wrapped around the earrings to help hold up the weight of the gold.

KENYA

Maasai Warrior

The Maasai people are constantly on the search for better grazing spots for their cattle, a quest that has kept them on the move across the grasslands of Kenya and Tanzania since the 15th century. The Maasai are cattle farmers and are known for their unique way of life, as well as for their distinctive traditional clothing.

The Maasai dress for each day's cattle herding with wrists and ankles stacked high with bracelets, colourful belts wrapped around their waists and an array of necklaces. One other accessory is an iron rod, carried to protect themselves from the threat of lion attacks as they travel across the vast savannah.

Maasai life is marked by three stages: childhood, warriorhood and elderhood. A Maasai boy reaches warriorhood around the age of 15 and can be recognised by his clothing and appearance. His hair is braided into intricate patterns, and he wears colourful jewellery to display his achievements. Maasai men's traditional robe, called a *shuka*, is usually bold red. The colour symbolises Maasai culture, and it is also believed that the hue is able to scare off lions, which would threaten their cattle. It is the warrior's job to protect the herd from harm. When the Maasai warrior reaches elderhood, he steps away from the day-to-day herding duties and takes on an advisory role — helping to make decisions that affect the whole community.

Each coloured bead is significant for the Maasai: blue reflects the colour of the sky and stands for their deity and green beads represent the earth and peace.

The red colour of the shuka is obtained by dyeing the fabric with natural pigments, like ochre (clay).

The Maasai originally made their jewellery out of seeds, stones and bones, all items easily found in their environment.

NAMIBIA

Herero Woman

Once nomads winding their way across the Kalahari Desert, the Herero people settled a few hundred years ago in sunburnt Namibia in Southern Africa and became cattle farmers. Today, the Herero still live in communities that form an arc around their cattle pens, protecting their beloved livestock from attack.

When it comes to their traditional dress of voluminous skirts and long-sleeved blouses, the Herero women believe the bigger, the better. On special occasions such as weddings and festivals, they add up to eight layers of colourful petticoats to make their skirts excessively wide, meant to represent the shape of their cattle. Each dress uses about nine metres of fabric. The sheer size of the dress also makes the women walk in a slow, swaying way, said to mimic the plodding movements of their cattle.

Yet it is their unique headdresses, called the *otjikaiva*, that truly shows how important the cattle are to the identity of the Herero people. Bright fabric is wound around and around the wearer's head, and fashioned into long points to represent a cow's horns. The Herero women even have smaller horn-shaped headdresses, which they often wear while they sleep.

Dresses made from patchwork are worn everyday, but dresses made from a single colour are reserved for special occasions, such as ceremonies.

The headdress often has a base made from rolled-up newspaper to help the fabric hold its shape.

It takes about one month to make the traditional dress. A Herero woman might have 18 or more dresses in her lifetime.

CAMEROON

Bamileke Masquerade Dancer

On a typical day in the fertile grasslands of western Cameroon, the Bamileke people spend their time tending to crops such as corn, yams and peanuts. But on special occasions, like ceremonies and funerals, the Bamileke put down their ploughs and put on an elaborate beaded costume, which includes an extraordinary mask that allows them to borrow the appearance of an elephant.

For the Bamileke, elephants signify wealth, power and royalty. For hundreds of years, the grasslands of Cameroon have been split into many different kingdoms — each ruled over by a different Bamileke king, called a *fon*. The Bamileke people believe their kings are so powerful, they can transform into an elephant at will and perform incredible feats of strength. Today at sacred masquerade festivals, the Bamileke people wear beaded elephant masks to honour their royal ancestors.

During the masquerade festival, Bamileke men perform an ancient ritual called *tso*, or 'the elephant dance'. As the dance begins, the beads and rattles attached to their clothing shake and produce a rhythmic sound. A long panel hangs from the mask and sways back and forth, like an elephant's trunk. The oversized pieces of fabric on either side of the mask flap in the air as if they were elephant ears. The Bamileke complete their masquerade clothing with a headdress of red feathers and a long robe, covered with beads and geometric symbols. The beads that adorn the clothing are rare and costly, and symbolise the power of the wearer and his kingdom.

The Bamileke use camwood to dye their clothing red. Red symbolises life and kingship in their community.

The geometric designs on the dancer's clothing represent leopard spots, another royal symbol in their culture.

Hundreds of thin tubes of black cloth make up the base of the headdress. Each ends in a single feather from the tail of the grey parrot, which symbolises leadership.

OCEANIA

Ten thousand islands dot the wide blue expanse of the southern Pacific Ocean, making up the region known as Oceania. Some of the islands are so tiny they measure just eight square miles across. Other rise precipitously like the spines of a half-submerged sea monster. In the west, Australia is the region's only continent, a land of sweltering deserts, crashing surf beaches and fertile river valleys.

While today's Oceanians wear modern styles, traditionally clothing was filled with symbolism. Though largely dependent on the materials they had to hand, since their neighbours were often an entire sea away, inhabitants were ingenious in their designs, weaving fabrics from flax and making tapa cloth out of tree bark. The importance of hair and anything associated with the head is a common thread that connects these islands, and often what is worn on the head is the most sacred element of all.

Aotearoa New Zealand

Māori Warrior

With a mighty stomping, the Māori warrior's knees are lifted high and land again with a ground-trembling thud. Their arms heave in sharp motions, tongues stuck out and flattened against their chins. This is the Māori haka, a ceremonial dance that can be used to welcome visitors, in celebrations and as a challenge. It is famously performed by New Zealand's All Blacks rugby team before their games.

Everything a Māori warrior wears to perform the haka helps to emphasise the movements of the dance. Their arms and torso are left free, or draped with a cloak crafted from feathers, to accentuate the Māori's sharp arm movements. Their lower half is wrapped in a *pari*, a kilt-like skirt woven from flax (a plant cultivated for its fibre and seeds), which makes a rustling sound as the performer stomps. Pendants made of pounamu (green jade) — a material that is treasured in Māori culture — hang from their neck. Curving lines of dark tattoos, called *moko*, follow the lines of their faces to make their fierce expressions look even more dramatic.

The head is the most sacred part of the body in Māori culture, so hair decoration is essential to complete the warrior's costume. Wood or bone combs, red titoki berries and clay are twisted into their hair in elaborate knot designs that reference traditional stories.

Each Māori face tattoo is personal to the performer, and tells the story of his family and culture.

Traditionally, high ranking Māori may have worn tail feathers from the huia in their hair. This sacred bird became extinct in the 20th century, mostly because of habitat loss and over-hunting by museum collectors.

Hei-tiki are neck pendants carved from stone or bone into human-like forms.

Papua New Guinea

Huli Wigman

Tucked among the rainforested peaks of Papua New Guinea live the Huli people. They believe that they are direct descendants of a male ancestor named Huli, who was the first man to have farmed in this hot, humid land. Today, the Huli people continue to take advantage of the fertile valleys of Papua New Guinea to raise pigs and grow vegetables, such as sweet potatoes.

The Huli's traditional clothing is instantly recognisable. The men wear arm and legbands and a cloth around their waists, accompanied by a fan of large leaves, known as *a---gras*, which is designed to mimic a bird's tail feathers. They complete their outfit by hanging strings of red beads and other ornaments around their necks.

The most important part of a Huli man's traditional dress is an elaborately decorated wig made of his own hair. The Huli take great pride in the creation of this headpiece. At age 14, boys leave home to stay in the house of a sacred wigman, who is believed to be have the power to make hair grow strong and fast. Splashing their hair with water three times a day, the boys sleep propped on an elbow and rest their necks on a log to prevent their precious hair from being flattened. After a year and a half, the hair is cut off and shaped into a wig. The wig is a symbol of the wearer's transition into adulthood and is usually worn for celebratory festivals, known as *singsings*.

To have constant access to water while growing their hair, the Huli usually live near a creek or a different water source. They are known to sing while sprinkling water onto their hair.

For special occasions, Huli men coat their faces in yellow clay, which is considered sacred in their culture. Red ochre clay is also worn by men who are considered to be warriors in the community.

For local ceremonies, wigs are often topped with a plume of feathers from a cassowary or bird of paradise.

SAMOA

Taupou Dancer

Oral histories tell that the two Pacific islands of Samoa were created by the god Tagaloa at the very beginning of time. Today on these islands, women called *taupou* perform an ancient dance called the *taualuga* at special ceremonies. Originally performed by a tribal chief's daughter to welcome important visitors, the dance has been sacred to the Samoan people for hundreds of years.

Today the *taualuga* is considered a symbol of the whole of Samoa, but still only a *taupou* is allowed to wear the traditional outfit created for this dance. The dress is made up of several layers of finely woven mats known as *'ie tōga* and is secured with a sash called a *vala*. The outfit is decorated with traditional designs and colourful feathers from the native birds of the islands. Around the neck, a *taupou* wears a boar's tusk or the teeth of whales.

On the top of a *taupou*'s head is the most important piece of all: a *tuiga*. The head is considered the most sacred part of the body in Samoan culture and the headdress is the crowning piece of this costume. Topped with tufts of hair bleached with seawater, nautilus shells and feathers, the *tuiga* is made up of some of Samoa's most prized materials — befitting for the dress of the chief's daughter. In the past, rare red feathers were as valuable to Samoan people as gold, and were used for trade with other islands in the South Pacific.

Europeans brought chickens to the islands in the 17th century and since then their feathers have often been used in place of human hair on the tuiga.

The dance begins with the taupou *twirling a nifo oti, a warrior club with a hooked blade.*

Originally woven into the taupou's hair, the tuiga *headdress can take 30 minutes to put on and is usually over 1m high.*

THE AUTHOR

Giovanna Alessio is a former staff writer at National Geographic magazine and an editor at National Geographic Books and the Smithsonian's Freer and Sackler galleries. She is a frequent contributor to National Geographic Kids, and has written for Scientific American, Newsweek and The Washington Post.

THE ILLUSTRATOR

Chaaya Prabhat is a graphic designer, illustrator and lettering artist. After completing her MA in Graphic Design from Savannah College of Art and Design, she is now working in Chennai, India. She has worked with several clients such as Snapchat, Facebook, Google and The Obama Foundation.

THE CONSULTANT

John Gillow has spent over thirty years studying, collecting and lecturing on textiles. His books include *World Textiles* (with Bryan Sentance), *Arts and Crafts of India* (with Ilay Cooper and Barry Dawson), *Indian Textiles* (with Nicholas Barnard), *Traditional Indonesian Textiles* and *African Textiles*.